This book belongs to:

TAILS FROM THE PANTRY

Little Life Lessons from Mom and Dad

Basil and Parsley

Other Books in the Tails from the Pantry Series

TAILS FROM THE PANTRY

Little Life Lessons from Mom and Dad

Basil and Parsley

By Patsy Clairmont

Illustrated by Joni Oeltjenbruns

Published by
THOMAS NELSON
Since 1798
www.thomasnelson.com

Library of Congress Cataloging-in-Publication Data

Clairmont, Patsy.
   Basil and Parsley / by Patsy Clairmont ; illustrated by Joni Oeltjenbruns.
      p. cm. — (Tails from the pantry)
   "Little life lessons from Mom and Dad."
   Summary: Basil and Parsley, twin mice that live in the pantry with the rest of
their family, are playing hide-and-seek when their older brother Stinky signals
that he is in trouble and the twins must work together to try to help him.
   ISBN-13: 978-1-4003-1039-5 (hardcover)
   ISBN-10: 1-4003-1039-3 (hardcover)
   [1. Twins—Fiction. 2. Brothers and sisters—Fiction. 3. Cooperativeness—
Fiction. 4. Mice—Fiction.] I. Oeltjenbruns, Joni, ill. II. Title.
PZ7.C5276Bas 2007
[E]—dc22
                                    2006036977

Printed in China
07 08 09 10 11 MT 5 4 3 2 1

**𝒯his little series is dedicated to
Justin and Noah. . . .**

How blessed I am to have two "little mouse" grandsons who regularly nibble in my pantry. Darlings, leave all the crumbs you want in Nana's house. I'll tidy up later. Always heed Mommy and Daddy's lessons about staying safe. You are both loved "a bushel and a peck and a hug around the neck."

~Nana

Once upon a pantry shelf hid two mice, Basil and Parsley, the MacKenzie twins. They loved to play games with their brothers and sister—Soccer, Stinky, and Meatball. Today it was Stinky's turn to entertain the twins because Meatball and Soccer were helping their mom carry groceries to the third shelf of the pantry, where they lived in a forgotten box of Christmas candy.

"Ready or not, here I come!" teased Stinky.

"Okay, Stinky, come find us!" Basil called out as he slid behind a can of black pepper.

"Yes, we're ready, Stinky," chimed in Parsley, who was curled up behind a jar of ginger.

The twins giggled with excitement.

Basil and Parsley waited, and waited, and waited, but Stinky didn't come.

"What's taking so long?" whispered Parsley.

"I dunno. Yoo-hoo, Stinky, come find us," called Basil. But there was no answer.

"Where do you think Stinky is, Basil?" Parsley asked with a quiver in her voice. She was worried about their brother.

"He's probably looking somewhere else. I'm sure he'll be here any minute," Basil answered.

"That's silly, Basil! Stinky knows where we are because we *always* hide in the same place."

Basil's ears perked up. "Oh, wait, I think I hear Stinky now. Listen."

Parsley heard something, too. It sounded like three knocks and a squeak.

"I think Stinky is in trouble, Parsley," Basil whispered.

"Really? Why?" Parsley asked, wide-eyed.

"Well, remember the day Daddy told us about emergency signals? He said if we ever get into trouble, we should tap three times over and over to let someone know where we are."

Basil and Parsley listened again.

Tap, tap, tap—squeak.

"What should we do, Basil?"

"I don't know," Basil admitted.

Tap, tap, tap—squeak.

Tap, tap, tap—squeak.

"Well," Parsley insisted, "we have to do something. Stinky needs us."

Basil thought for a minute. "Look, Parsley, what if we take turns helping each other up onto the cans until we reach the next shelf? C'mon, I'll show you."

Basil knelt down. He told Parsley to stand on his back and then crawl up onto the can of tuna fish.

Parsley did what her brother said. "Now what?" she called down to Basil.

"Uh, I don't know. I can't jump that high without a boost," Basil confessed after trying several times.

"Why don't you nibble into that bag of marshmallows and roll one over to stand on."

"Good idea, Sister."

Basil nibbled away, and in no time he had made a hole big enough to pull out a marshmallow. He rolled it over to the tuna fish can; then he climbed onto it and pulled himself up beside Parsley.

Parsley stared up at the next can, which was even higher than the last. "Basil, how do we get up there?"

"Uh-oh, now *that's* a problem," Basil admitted.

Tap, tap, tap—squeak.

Tap, tap, tap—squeak.

"I know what we can do. Basil, go back down and get that empty mesh bag. Then nibble your way into that bag of spaghetti and hand up a few noodles. Oh, yes, and see those miniature marshmallows over there? Stick a couple of them in your pockets."

Basil went lickety-split and soon returned with the bag, the spaghetti, and the marshmallows. "Now what?" Basil huffed, out of breath from all the pulling and tugging.

"Well, we could throw the bag up in front of a can and scale it like rock climbers do."

Tap, tap, tap—squeak.

"C'mon, Sister, we've got to hurry!"

Parsley and Basil threaded the spaghetti strands through the open weave of the bag and then leaned it up against a can of corn.

"Okay, Parsley, you go first."

Parsley began scaling the bag. Higher and higher and higher she climbed, until she finally pulled herself up onto the can of corn. She peeked over the side to let Basil know she was safe, but looking down made her feel funny inside her tummy.

"I'm almost there," Basil called out, "but I need a hand to get up on the can."

"I can't look over the side, Basil. It makes the butterflies in my tummy flutter."

"Just hold out your hand and don't look down," Basil instructed. "When I grab your hand, pull as hard as you can." Parsley pulled hard until . . . *thump* . . . Basil was on the can beside her. They sat there together, looking at the shelf above their heads. Then Parsley began to cry. "Oh, Basil, what can we do? I'm so worried about Stinky!"

Basil thought and thought. Finally, it came to him. He pulled the marshmallows out of his pockets and tucked one under each foot.

"I really wanted to eat those marshmallows," Parsley confessed, "but it looks like you have a better idea."

Basil stood on his tippytoes, stretched his hands up to the edge of the shelf, and grabbed with all his might. But his hands slipped, and he tumbled back down and disappeared right over the edge of the shelf.

"Basil!" Parsley screamed.

Parsley peered over the scary edge. She couldn't believe her eyes. On the shelf below stood Spud the bully rat, holding Basil in his outstretched arms. Parsley didn't know if she should jump for joy or scream for help.

Then Spud did the nicest thing. Without a word, he put Basil on his shoulders and jumped onto the shelf where Parsley was. Now from Spud's shoulders, Basil safely stepped onto the next shelf. Spud helped Parsley do the same thing. After a stunned "Thank you!" from the twins, Spud tipped his baseball cap and headed back down, disappearing as quickly as he had come.

Basil and Parsley hugged. They couldn't believe Spud the bully had rescued them. Just then, they heard the taps again. They sounded much closer now.

Tap, tap, tap—squeak.

"Stinky? Stinky?" Parsley called.

"Here I am," Stinky called out. "Help me!"

The twins ran behind a pickle jar, and there was Stinky with the tip of his tail caught in a mousetrap.

"Oh, Stinky, how can we get you out of that mousetrap?" Basil asked.

"See that spoon over by the sugar bowl? You and Parsley will have to use it to pry open the metal piece that's holding my tail."

In a jiffy the twins pulled the spoon over and carefully slipped the tip of the spoon handle under the metal. They both hung on to the bowl of the spoon and pushed down as hard as they could, and finally the clamp moved just enough to free Stinky's tail.

Stinky gave the twins a big hug. "Boy, am I glad you found me," he said, holding his throbbing tail. "Let's go home."

At dinner that evening, Basil, Parsley, and Stinky shared their adventures with their family. Daddy asked them each to tell something they had learned that day. Basil was first.

"I learned that sometimes even a bully like Spud can be kind."

Parsley was next. "I learned that it's a lot easier to solve problems when we work together, like Basil and I did," she said.

Finally it was Stinky's turn. "Well, Dad, I learned that it's good to know how to signal for help when you're in trouble and also . . . that I'd rather be *part* of an adventurous tale than *lose* a tail!"